City Dog

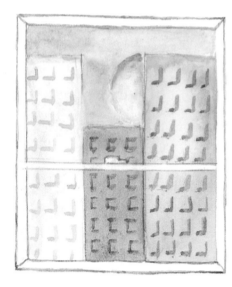

City Dog

Written and Illustrated by
Karla Kuskin

CLARION BOOKS / *New York*

Clarion Books
a Houghton Mifflin Company imprint
215 Park Avenue South, New York, NY 10003
Text and illustrations copyright © 1994 by Karla Kuskin

Illustrations executed in watercolor on Winsor & Newton watercolor paper
Text is set in 22/30 pt Optima

Printed in Singapore

Library of Congress Cataloging-in-Publication Data

Kuskin, Karla.
City dog / by Karla Kuskin
p.   cm.
Summary: A rhyming tale of a city dog's first outing in the country.
ISBN: 0-395-66138-2   PA ISBN: 0-395-90016-6
[1. Dogs—Fiction. 2. Nature—Fiction. 3. Stories in rhyme.] I. Title.
PZ8.3.K96Ci   1994
[E]—dc20   93-8252
CIP
AC

TWP   10

For Madeleine Margaret with love.

We took the dog

to the country

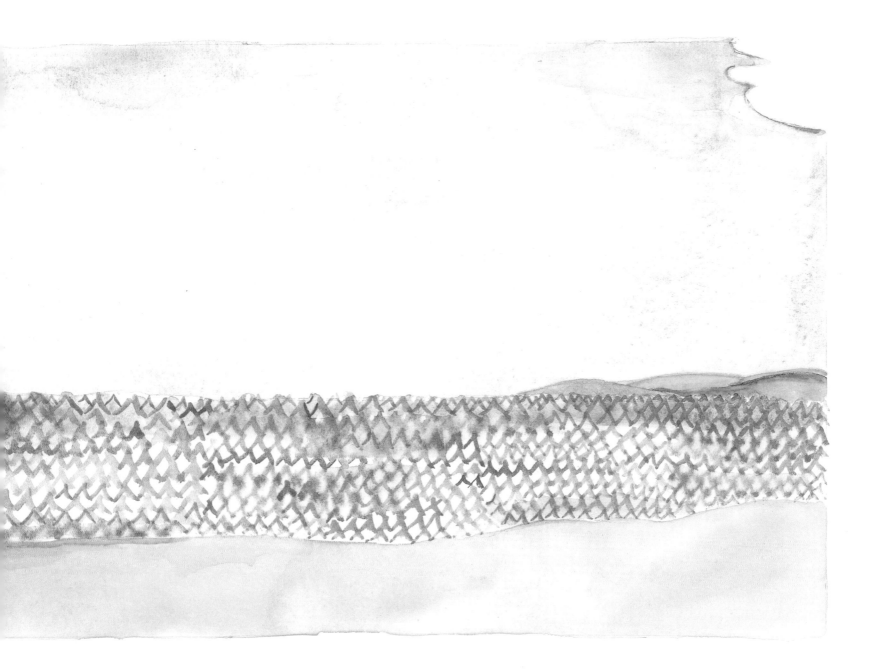

and she didn't know when to stop walking

she didn't know when to stop barking.

She looked for the blocks
she looked for the streets
those corners
where city dogs mingle and meet.

But there weren't any sidewalks
no drugstores
no bounds . . .

...nothing but country-side rolling around.

Soft grass
warm ground
rabbit holes
to paw and nose
fast bikes
bare toes.

Blue waves
crabs
crows.

And when the red sun
fell behind the hills
into the sea
everybody
(you and me)
went home
the birds
the boats.

And soon a yellow melon moon rose up above the wind
and lit the road, trees, oats.

And she
the city dog,
skipped out
drinking dark air
feeling a little wild

while floating in the middle of the night
the melon yellow moon looked down
at the pretty city dog
kicking up the countryside,
        and smiled.

We took the dog to the country
and she didn't know when to stop walking
she didn't know when to stop barking.

She looked for the blocks
she looked for the streets
those corners
where city dogs mingle and meet.

But there weren't any sidewalks
no drugstores
no bounds . . .
nothing but countryside rolling around.

Soft grass
warm ground
rabbit holes
to paw and nose
fast bikes
bare toes.

Blue waves
crabs
crows.

And when the red sun
fell behind the hills
into the sea
everybody
(you and me)
went home
the birds
the boats.

And soon a yellow melon moon rose up
above the wind
and lit the road, trees, oats.

And she
the city dog,
skipped out
drinking dark air
feeling a little wild

while floating in the middle of the night
the melon yellow moon looked down
at the pretty city dog
kicking up the countryside,
                 and smiled.